MEDICI BOOKS FOR CHILDREN

RICHARD RA.
GOES BOATING

Written and illustrated by Truda Mordue

"I say", said young Richard Rabbit to his four brothers, "Look at Sam and Sid Squirrel scratching about on the ground near the fence. Let's go and see what they are doing!"

"Yes, let's," said the brothers who always did anything Richard told them to do.

They ran over to the squirrels, and found them burying acorns, sweet chestnuts and hazel nuts.

The rabbits watched them for a little while, but the squirrels took no notice of them. "What a silly thing to be doing!" said Richard at last, "I suppose you've nothing better to do."

"Oh, go away and mind your own business!" barked Sam Squirrel, "We are only putting food away for the winter, and that's not a silly thing to be doing, surely."

Sid Squirrel looked up and said crossly, "Have you Rabbits nothing better to do than annoy us when we are busy?"

At that moment Mother Rabbit came running towards them, calling, "Children, take cover! I've just heard that a weasel is snooping about near here. Be quick, and go indoors!"

"Ha! Ha!", laughed Richard, "We're not afraid of a little weasel, are we, lads?"

"N-no, we're n-not afraid," said the others, trembling with fright. The squirrels fled towards a tree.

"Don't be so stupid, Richard," said Mother severely, "Weasels are dangerous, so come home at once!"

Richard then did as he was told, and ran back to the warren with his brothers.

The squirrels darted up the tree, and hid in the branches.

The animals had hidden just in time as the weasel had got fairly close to them, and if they hadn't heeded Mother Rabbit's warning, Weasel might have had one of them for his dinner!

Suddenly, a jay, perched overhead in a tree, made some very loud squawks. The noise alarmed Weasel so much that he ran off as fast as he could go.

Weasel kept on running, and as he ran he wondered what kind of monster made those dreadful sounds, and if it was coming after him. After crossing three fields, Weasel halted.

He looked behind him and seeing no monster following him, he trotted on until he reached the bank of a river.

The squirrels in the tree had watched Weasel running until he was out of sight, and then they hopped down to the ground.

Sam Squirrel called out to the rabbits, "It's all right, you can all come out to play again. Weasel's gone a long way from here."

The rabbits came out from the warren, hopping merrily.

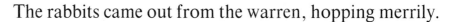

The animals were playing a jolly game, when Richard had a bright idea. He asked, "Don't you think it would be a nice change to go down to the riverside and watch the herons and kingfishers fishing?"

"Good idea!", agreed the others. So off they all scampered, and soon reached the river bank.

Tied to a post was a small rowing-boat, and Richard hopped inside.

"Come along, jump in!" he cried, "This boat makes a fine grandstand."

The animals followed Richard, and lined themselves up on the boat's edge, but they had not noticed that a water-vole was gnawing at the boat's rope!

They were much too interested in a kingfisher diving after fish!

The water-vole was simply amusing itself, and gnawed happily through the rope until it broke, causing the boat to drift away from the bank.

Richard was the first to notice that their "grandstand" was moving away downstream.

"Hi!" shouted Richard, "Somebody's cut the boat's rope, and we're adrift!"

"Oh dear! So we are! Can't you stop the boat drifting?" cried the animals, who always depended on clever Richard to get them out of trouble.

The boat continued to drift, and the poor little animals became quite scared.

Richard was also frightened, but he put on a brave face.

"Don't worry, everything will be all right," said he, but the others were not so sure, and squealed at Richard, "It's all your doing, you're always getting us into scrapes!"

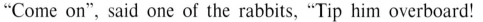

"Come on", said one of the rabbits, "Tip him overboard! That'll teach him a lesson!" But Richard was saved from a ducking, for, at that moment, the boat gave a jerk as it stopped in dense-growing reeds.

"Goodness! Now we are badly caught in the reeds!" cried Sam Squirrel, "You've got us into this mess, clever Richard, now get us out of it!"

"Oh, *do* stop moaning", said Richard, "We'll get away. See that oar? Well, I'm going to use it to push the boat away from the reeds, and get us all back to the bank."

As Richard was pointing to the oar, two otters came up to the boat, and called out, "Hi there! Watch out for a weasel creeping along the bank. He's coming towards the boat!"

"It must be that horrid Weasel again!", cried Richard, "Now he's got us trapped."

"Oh, we're trapped, and we've heard that weasels can swim," wailed the other animals.

But they were saved again, as a dog came running along the towpath barking loudly, with its owner following in the distance.

The dog headed straight for Weasel, who gave one look at the big animal, and then darted away to find a safer place to hunt.

Richard saw what had happened, and called to the others, "It's all right now! The dog has chased Weasel away, and I can try to get the boat moving. Sam, you can help me lift up the oar."

Richard and Sam Squirrel, with the help of the otters, managed to push the boat away from the reeds and get it to the bank. The animals were then able to leave their "grandstand" and they reached their warren in time for supper.

As Richard munched a lettuce leaf, he said to his brothers, "I bet you are all glad that you didn't throw me overboard!"

Several weeks passed, and winter had arrived. Snow covered the ground, and the young rabbits were out having lots of fun.

The squirrels in the tree were enjoying the sunshine. "I'm hungry," said Sam. "Me too," said Sid, "Let's find something to eat." They skipped down to the ground.

"Can you remember where we buried those nuts?" asked Sam.

"Oh dear, I've forgotten!" cried Sid, "Wasn't it under the tree?"

They scooped away the snow, and dug around, but found no nuts. Suddenly Sam uncovered something very prickly from under a heap of leaves. "Whatever is that?" asked Sid, "Look out, it's moving!" But it was only Mr Hedgehog, who scolded them for disturbing his sleep.

Richard suddenly noticed the squirrels, and shouted "Look at the squirrels tossing snow everywhere!" The rabbits ran over to the squirrels and found them in tears. "What's the matter?" asked Richard.

"We can't find those nuts we buried, and we are so hungry," they wailed.

"I remember where you buried them," said clever Richard, "over there by the fence. Come on lads, we'll help them find those nuts!"

The rabbits soon uncovered enough food for the squirrels to have a good meal.

"Thanks a lot for finding our food for us," said Sam, "We squirrels have rather bad memories, I'm afraid."

"Glad we could help you," said Richard, "And now let's all have a lovely time playing in the snow before it melts away."